WE'RE OFF TO LOOK FOR
ALIENS

Colin Mc Naughton

WALKER BOOKS
AND SUBSIDIARIES
LONDON · BOSTON · SYDNEY · AUCKLAND

We're off to look for aliens,
Ugly-bugly aliens,
We're off to look for aliens,
Wilberforce and I.

We built a little rocket ship,
A rocket ship, a pocket ship.
We built a little rocket ship,
Wilberforce and I.

To all our friends we said, "Goodbye."
Said, "Goodbye, we must fly."
We blasted off into the sky,
Wilberforce and I.

Around the moon and to the stars,
To the stars! To the stars!
We landed on the planet Mars,
Wilberforce and I.

Planet Mars was hot and dry,
We looked a Martian in the eye.
We said hello and said goodbye,
Wilberforce and I.

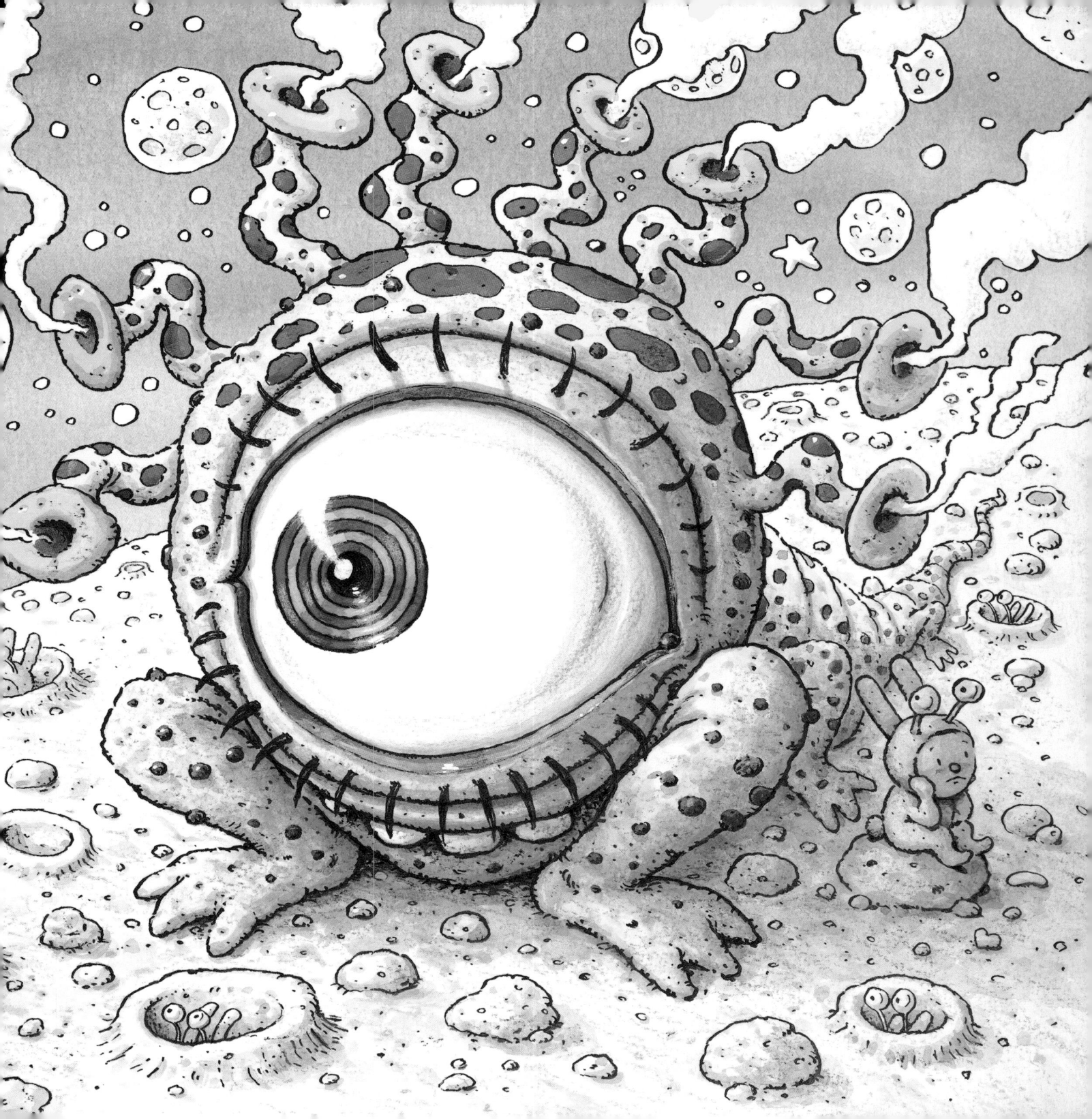

"Here we go round the universe,
The universe, the universe.
Here we go round the universe,
Wilberforce and I."

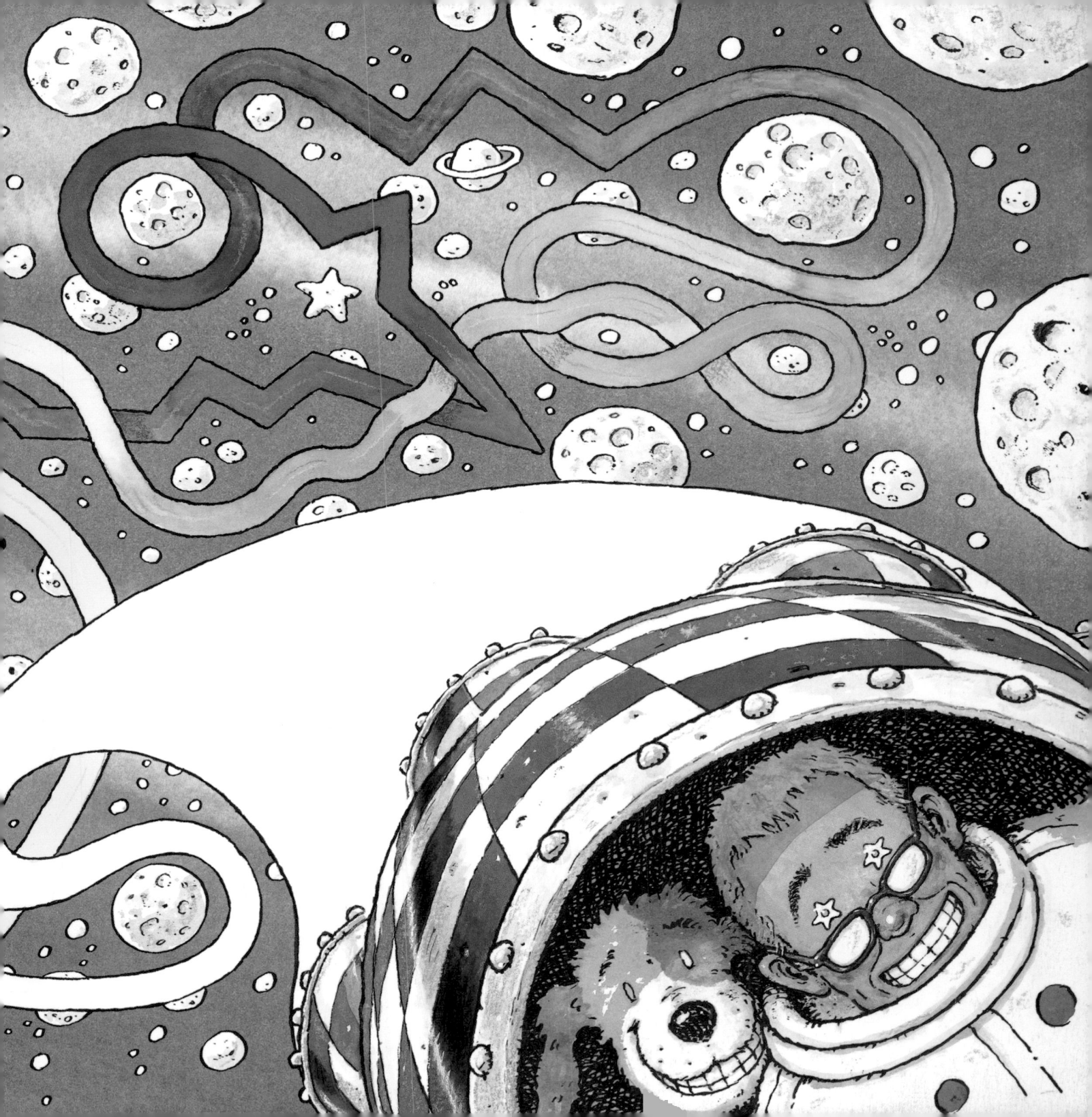

These beings came in different sizes,
Different guises, different sizes.
We were in for some surprises,
Wilberforce and I.

We saw lots of smelly things,
Never-seen-on-telly things.
Eyeballs-in-their-belly things,
Wilberforce and I.

Some were cold and some were hot,
Some were tall and some were squat.
We were friendly (they were not!),
Wilberforce and I.

We weren't welcome anywhere.
And we were running out of air,
Just one more planet – over there,
Wilberforce and I.

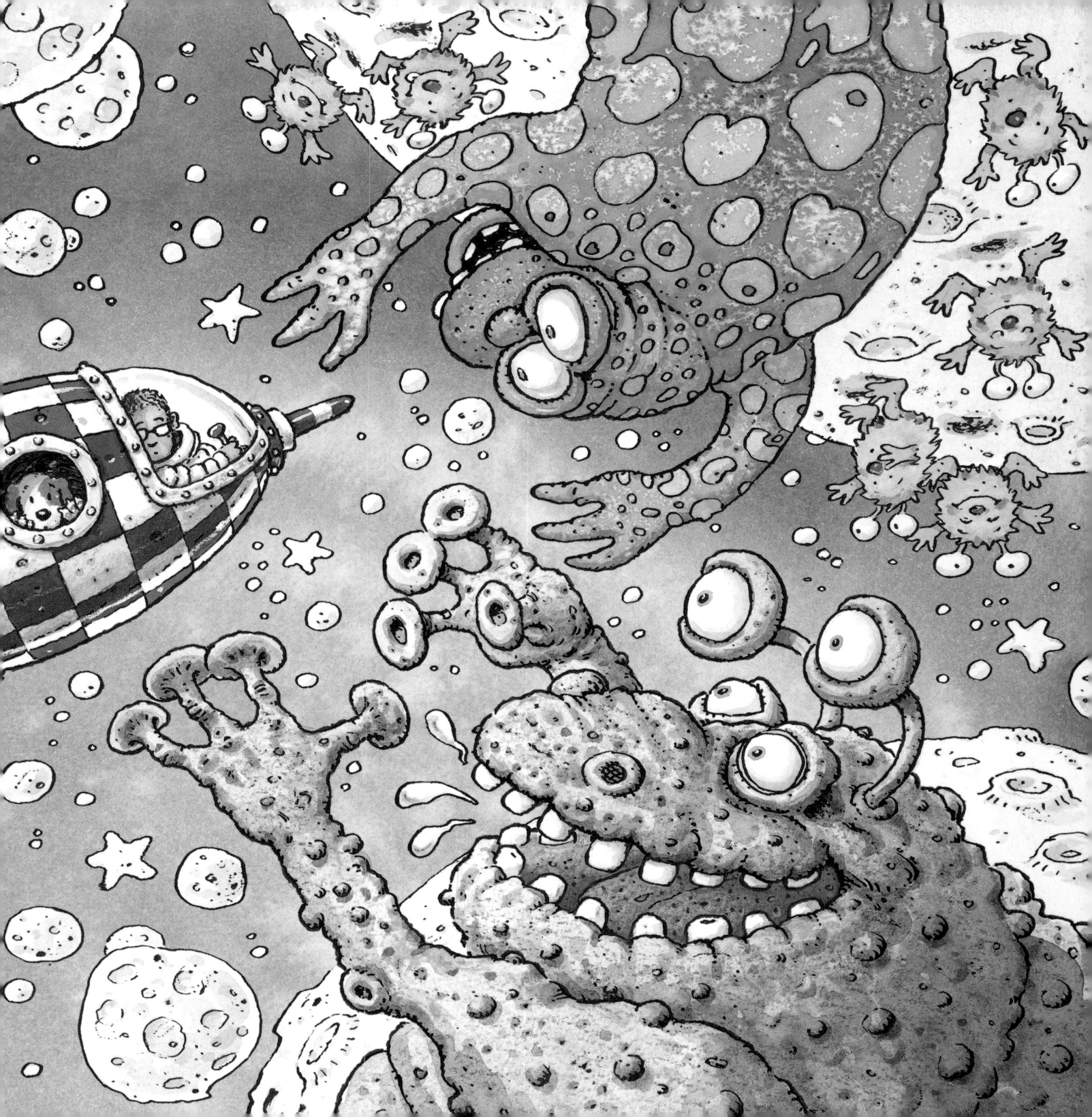

There we met an alien girl,
An alien girl, an alien girl.
We met a lovely alien girl,
Wilberforce and I.

I fell in love and took her home,
Took her home, took her home.
We blasted off and took her home,
Wilberforce and I.

We landed safely, hip-hooray!
Hip-hooray! Hip-hooray!
A little bump, but all okay,
Wilberforce, the alien girl and I.

And we were happy ever after,
Full of laughter, ever after.
We were happy ever after -
in a whirl,
my alien girl.
What a joy,
a baby boy.
Then another,
baby brother.
And of course,
Wilberforce - and I.

The End